Uranus and the Bubbles of Trouble

HEROES IN TRAINING

Uranus and the Bubbles of Trouble

Joan Holub and
Suzanne Williams

Aladdin NEW YORK LONDON TORONTO SYDNEY NEW DELHI

ALADDIN

An imprint of Simon & Schuster Children's Publishing Division
1230 Avenue of the Americas, New York, NY 10020
First Aladdin hardcover edition December 2015
Text copyright © 2015 by Joan Holub and Suzanne Williams
Illustrations copyright © 2015 by Craig Phillips
Also available in an Aladdin paperback edition.
All rights reserved, including the right of reproduction
in whole or in part in any form.
ALADDIN is a trademark of Simon & Schuster, Inc.,
and related logo is a registered trademark of Simon & Schuster, Inc.
For information about special discounts for bulk purchases,
please contact Simon & Schuster Special Sales
at 1-866-506-1949 or business@simonandschuster.com.
The Simon & Schuster Speakers Bureau can bring authors to your live event.
For more information or to book an event,
contact the Simon & Schuster Speakers Bureau at 1-866-248-3049
or visit our website at www.simonspeakers.com.
Series designed by Karin Paprocki
Jacket designed by Karina Granda
Interior designed by Mike Rosamilia
The text of this book was set in Adobe Garamond Pro.
Manufactured in the United States of America 1015 FFG
2 4 6 8 10 9 7 5 3 1
Library of Congress Control Number 2015952119
ISBN 978-1-4814-3513-0 (hc)
ISBN 978-1-4814-3512-3 (pbk)
ISBN 978-1-4814-3514-7 (eBook)

For our heroic readers:
Wyatt B., Sebastian C., Anh H., Jenny G., Luke O.,
Sophia O., Harper M., Parker M., the Andrade Family,
Lily-Ann and Daddy, Ann S., Christine D.-H.,
Kenzo S., Julio A., Lucas A., Caitlin R., Hannah R.,
Joey W., Mackenzie and Ivan S., Amanda W., Landon H.,
Trey H., Steele H., and you!
—J. H. and S. W.

⚡ Contents ⚡

Uranus and the Bubbles of Trouble

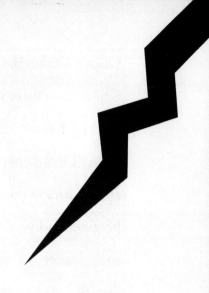

Greetings,
Mortal Readers,

I am Pythia, the Oracle of Delphi, in Greece. I have the power to see the future. Hear my prophecy:

Ahead, I see dancers lurking. Wait—make that *danger* lurking. (The future can be blurry, especially when my eyeglasses are foggy.)

Anyhoo, beware! Titan giants seek to rule all of Earth's domains—oceans, mountains, forests, and the depths of the Underwear.

Oops—make that *Underworld*. Led by King Cronus, they are out to destroy us all!

Yet I foresee hope. A band of rightful rulers called Olympians will arise. Though their size and youth are no match for the Titans, they will be giant in heart, mind, and spirit. They await their leader—a very special boy. One who is destined to become king of the gods and ruler of the heavens.

If he is brave enough.

And if he and his friends work together as one. And if they can learn to use their new amazing flowers—um, amazing *powers*—in time to save the world!

CHAPTER ONE

The Ruler of the Sky

Ten-year-old Zeus and his band of ten Olympians stood on an island in the Aegean Sea and craned their necks to stare upward. The sky above them had started to turn as black as night—in the middle of the day! Obviously, this was no ordinary darkness.

"Guys, this doesn't look good," he said. The others—all kids Zeus's own age—nodded gravely. They had been gathering coconuts and berries before setting sail in a ship they'd stolen—um, borrowed.

"Yeah, something's not right," agreed his curly-haired brother Hades. "We just went from day to night in a few minutes!"

"It's like time sped up," added their red-haired sister, Demeter.

Besides Zeus, Hades, and Demeter, the Olympian members included another brother named Poseidon, and sisters Hera and Hestia. Onshore nearby were also Apollo and his twin sister, Artemis. With Athena, Ares, and the newest member, Hephaestus, that made eleven Olympians in all.

Black-haired, blue-eyed Zeus was the leader of the group. Though he and the others looked like normal mortal boys and girls, they were actually immortals and their actions were mighty. And they were absolutely determined to stop their giant enemies, the evil King Cronus (ruler of the Titans) and his Crony henchmen, from taking over the world. This was an outcome every citizen in Greece lived in fear of!

What the sudden strange sky had to do with Cronus, Zeus wasn't sure. But he guessed there must be some connection. No sooner did he think this than a deep voice boomed from overhead.

"I am Uranus, ruler of the sky!"

Zeus froze. Because Uranus's voice sounded oddly familiar. Also, because the sky didn't usually talk.

Poseidon—the god of the sea—jabbed Zeus in the shoulder with his magical three-pronged trident, jolting him from his frozen state. "Which guy?" Poseidon asked, confusion showing in his turquoise-blue eyes.

"Guy? What do you mean?" Now it was Zeus's turn to be confused.

"He said he was ruler of 'this guy,'" Poseidon replied. "So, which guy?"

Zeus sighed. "Ruler of *the sky*," he corrected Poseidon impatiently.

Hera leaned over to them. "Another Titan, do you think?"

Before anyone could reply, Uranus took shape in the darkness above them. The Olympians stared at him in awe.

He was massive, bigger than any Titan they had ever seen. His dark-blue form filled the entire sky, arching from one end of the horizon to the other. Stars glittered across his body. He had a white face and beard, and his eyes twinkled with piercing starlight.

"Behold my grandness! For I am the greatest of your enemies, the Titans!" Uranus boomed in answer to Hera's question. "The biggest, baddest daddy of them all! Fear me if you know what's good for you."

Zeus bravely stepped forward. "You want us to fear you?"

Uranus nodded his enormous head. "And I want you to fear him, too," he added, gesturing toward something beyond the Olympians.

They whipped around to see what—or who— Uranus was talking about. Behind them on the island's highest hill stood King Cronus!

"Butt out. I can handle this myself, Father!" Cronus yelled up to Uranus in an irritated voice.

Father?

"That's it!" Zeus snapped his fingers. "I knew Uranus's voice sounded familiar. He sounds like Cronus."

King Cronus was Zeus's *father*. Which made this amazing Uranus guy Zeus's *grandfather*!

They were father and grandfather to Zeus's brothers and sisters too. But none of them knew it yet. Zeus hadn't had the heart to tell them their enemy was also their dad!

Poseidon was staring at Uranus. "Wow! Who knew there was such a gigantic being? So should we fear him like he asked?"

Zeus gestured toward Cronus. "We've got other, closer Titans to fear right now, don't you think?"

"I'm not sure which is worse," said Hades, eyeing both Titans.

"Yeah, a guy as big as a sky could catch us pretty fast, no matter where we run," agreed Hestia.

Zeus hated to call Cronus's attention back to himself and the other Olympians, but there was something he needed to know. "Cronus! Where is our mother?" he called out, hoping his voice would reach his father's giant ears.

"Yeah, good question. Where is Rhea?" Artemis demanded, glancing around at her siblings.

Cronus had captured Rhea and was keeping her away from her Olympian children. In fact, the evil king had even swallowed some of Zeus's brothers and sisters a while back! He'd kept them in his giant belly for years until Zeus had rescued them by forcing Cronus to barf them up.

But Cronus didn't hear them. As he and his dad had begun to argue, a stormy wind had suddenly whipped up between them, fueled by their fury.

"As usual, you've made a mess of things," Uranus scolded his son. "Leaving *me* to step in. You are a disappointment and a failure!"

"Am NOT!" Cronus shot back angrily. Then in a pouty voice he added, "You've always liked my brothers and sisters better than me!"

With a swish of her blond ponytail, Hera ran over to Zeus. "Are we just going to stand here while these two argue?" she demanded. "Or are we going to try to escape? We have a ship, you know."

The Olympians had taken the ship for transport after an oracle named Pythia had sent them here on a quest. She was always sending them on quests—usually to locate more Olympians and various magical objects that would help them battle their enemies. She always gave them a clue telling them what to look for—but often, her foggy spectacles meant the clues were a little off. *Find the bubbles,* she had said this last time, just before disappearing into the hazy mist that always surrounded her.

Bubbles? What bubbles? Like most of Pythia's instructions, it didn't make much sense. So it was up to the Olympians to discover what Pythia had really meant.

Hephaestus's dark hair whipped in the wind as he spoke up now. "I think we should scram, but unfortunately, *I'm* not in charge here," he said in a voice that clearly indicated he *wanted* to be the Olympians' leader.

"Don't be ridiculous!" Zeus heard Uranus bellow at Cronus over the storm they'd stirred up. "I've always given you just as much attention as any of your siblings. More, in fact!"

"Yes, but only to *criticize* me," Cronus said peevishly.

"Hera's right. Let's scram." Zeus nudged the others and began sidling toward the ship.

SPLASH! Suddenly, a huge wave crashed against the shore, causing the ship to sway. The Olympians froze in their tracks as water swirled inland. If the ropes that held their ship fast came untied, they would lose their transportation!

"Look! It's Oceanus making waves!" Poseidon pointed toward the sea, where a huge figure was rising. Oceanus was another Titan, one with golden skin, long hair, and a beard that flowed down his face like the waves. They had battled Oceanus once before—and won. Or so they'd thought.

"What is this? A Titan family reunion?" grumped Hera.

His eyes blazing, Oceanus looked up at his father, Uranus. "The Olympians are mine!" He thrashed his long, thick serpentine tail, which sent another wave crashing against the shore and caused the Olympian's ship to bob up and down even harder.

Uranus laughed. "You had your chance to destroy them and failed." He pointed to the trident Poseidon had won from Oceanus in their previous battle. Poseidon quickly thrust it out of sight behind his back.

"And, Cronus, you could not even keep your own children in your belly after you swallowed them." Hearing this, Poseidon, Hera, Hades, Hestia, and Demeter all gasped. They were the five who'd been swallowed.

"Children? Fiddling fish sticks!" cried Poseidon. "That must mean that Cronus is our . . . *dad*?" All the Olympians glanced in confusion at Zeus.

"Did you know about this?" Hera demanded.

CHAPTER TWO

Who's Ruling Who?

U m . . . yeah," Zeus admitted. "Cronus told me during our battle back when he was building Mount Titan."

Ares glared at Zeus. "And when were you planning to tell us?"

"I . . . I don't know. The whole thing was so weird," Zeus admitted. "I still haven't gotten used to the idea myself. And I didn't know *how* to tell you. I guess I was waiting for just the right moment, and—"

"Really?" Hera interrupted, her blue eyes flashing with anger. "The right moment was about *three quests ago*, you Boltbrain!"

A strong gust of wind blew across the shore just then, nearly knocking the Olympians off their feet. Was it just his imagination, wondered Zeus, or was the storm getting stronger as the Titans' argument got worse?

"I kept those Olympian brats in my belly for years!" Cronus yelled to Uranus and Oceanus. Then he pointed Zeus's way. "Losing them was this blasted Barf Boy's fault!"

"Yet you haven't recaptured them. For every additional moment the Olympians roam free, mortals mock you," Uranus scolded. "You know the prophecy—a child of yours shall take your place as the ruler of all!"

The Olympians looked at one another in sur-prise. Then Hera glared at Zeus. "Did you—"

"No! I did not know that," Zeus defended himself.

"Wait, so *one* of us will be the ruler of every-thing?" Poseidon asked. "I thought we were *all* going to rule together. Like a team."

"I think he's talking about the ruler of the Earth realm," said Hades. "You know, like how I already rule the Underworld, and you rule the sea."

"Yeah, but he made it sound like the Earth realm is more important than the Underworld or the sea," Poseidon said unhappily.

Everyone looked at Zeus again. Since he was the Olympians' leader and had freed his siblings from Cronus's belly, it seemed likely the proph-ecy referred to him.

"Why do boys always get to rule everything?" Hera complained.

"I don't think that's true," gray-eyed Athena consoled her. "I rule cleverness. And Hestia rules the fires of the hearth, and Demeter rules the plants, right?"

Artemis raised her bow and arrow high. "And I rule the hunt!"

Red-eyed Ares clenched his fists in anger. Looking ready to explode, he blurted, "So what do I rule? Spears?"

"Calm down, crankypants," said Hera.

Zeus glanced around at the fighting Titan trio as the winds grew stronger yet. Caught between Uranus in the sky, Oceanus in the sea, and Cronus on a hilltop not far away, the Olympians were sitting ducks. And as soon as the Titans stopped arguing long enough to realize that, Zeus and his friends would be toast!

Oops, too late, Zeus thought as Uranus pointed down at the Olympians.

"Here they stand on this island, and yet you do nothing!" Uranus taunted Cronus. "What are you two boys waiting for? Crush them!"

With a mighty roar Oceanus dove back into the ocean. Cronus stomped off. Both were heading for the Olympians, meaning to do them harm.

"What now, fearless leader?" Hera asked Zeus.

"Escape! To the ship!" Zeus cried.

"Yeah, like I suggested before," added Hera, rolling her eyes.

The eleven Olympians splashed into the sea and scrambled aboard their ship. Ares, Artemis, Hades, and Hestia each grabbed a long oar. Zeus and the others worked the sails and ship's wheel. As they pushed off, an enormous wave broke against the side of their vessel, nearly tipping it over. Luckily, they managed to right it and sail away.

They were far from safe, however. Suddenly, the huge, shaggy head of Oceanus rose up from the water behind them. A hand reached out.

Quickly, Zeus removed the thunderbolt-shaped dagger from his belt. Bolt was a magical object. He had pulled it from a stone in the Temple at Delphi, and it had helped him fight dozens of dastardly creatures ever since.

"Bolt, large!" Zeus cried. At his command, the thunderbolt grew as tall as he was and glowed with bright, white light. "Attack!" Zeus yelled, throwing it into the sky. He had a plan. And he was aiming for bigger prey than Oceanus. *Much* bigger.

Bolt disappeared into the darkness that stretched overhead. Then . . .

BOOM! A thunderous explosion rocked the sky.

Uranus stared in shock at Cronus. "Did you

just attack me?" As Zeus had hoped, Uranus had been so focused on criticizing both his sons that he hadn't noticed what Zeus was up to.

"Ha!" Cronus yelled back. "You always blame me. Why not suspect the Olympians or Oceanus?"

"I didn't do anything," grouched Oceanus.

Doesn't anybody in this family get along? Zeus wondered. But at least their argument was allowing the Olympians to make a getaway.

Enraged, Cronus began chunking rocks at his father and brother. Uranus fought back, producing stars that appeared sharper and more dangerous than any stars the Olympians had ever seen in the sky, and hurling them at his sons!

Snap! Crackle! Pop! Broken stars and rocks rained down from the sky.

"Duck!" Hades yelled. The Olympians scrambled to find cover as some of the broken pieces hit the ship's deck.

Uranus sent another star hurtling toward Cronus, but the strong wind blew it off-course. It wound up smacking Oceanus in the head instead. "Ow!" yelped the watery Titan.

"Good shot!" Ares cheered as Oceanus turned tail and swam away, fleeing the chaos.

"Ha-ha! Scaredy-serpent!" teased Poseidon.

"Everybody keep us moving! They won't forget about us for long," Zeus said, anxiously eyeing the two remaining Titans, one on the island hill and one overhead. He grabbed the oval, smooth chip of stone that he wore on a cord around his neck. Like Bolt, Chip was a magical object too. One that always managed to steer them toward the right path and away from danger.

"Chip, get us out of here!" Zeus commanded. "Take us to the bubbles!"

CHAPTER THREE

An Ocean of Trouble

The Olympians' ship zoomed onward in the direction of Chip's black compass-like arrow. Then suddenly Chip's arrow began to glow green and spin crazily.

Poseidon stared at it in surprise. "What's wrong with that thing?"

Athena studied the churning waves surrounding the boat. "The Titans' anger is whipping up the sea. I'm guessing these frothy air bubbles in the water are confusing Chip. He must think they're the bubbles Pythia wants us to find."

"Maybe they are," suggested Zeus. Pythia hadn't explained what kind of bubbles they were supposed to find or what they were supposed to do once they found them. Typical!

"Hmph! Forget Chip! My feather will help us." Hera held out her magical object, a peacock feather. "Feather, feather, can you see, a safer place for us to be?" She had to speak in rhyme or it wouldn't obey her. Normally, she would have let her feather fly off to search for such a safe place. But afraid of losing it in the wind, she held it tightly now.

She gazed into its eye as an image began to form there. "I see another island! I'll ask my feather to lead us there."

But before she could do that, Chip spoke up. It had its own special language, Chip Latin.

It was like pig Latin, only you moved the first letter of each word to the end of the word and added "ip."

"O-nip! Tay-sip at-ip ea-sip!" Chip said.

"What did it say?" Hephaestus asked, raising his eyebrows.

"It told us to stay at sea," Zeus translated.

"But the image on my feather is telling us to go ashore," Hera argued.

Poseidon shook his head. "You and Zeus hardly ever agree on anything. And now your magical objects can't agree either!"

Fighting against the wind, Hera marched over to the sails and grabbed the ropes. "My feather's right! We'll find those bubbles at the coast!" she announced. She pulled at the ropes with all her might but couldn't shift the sails. "A little help here!" she called out, when no one moved to assist her.

Zeus was a little annoyed that Hera was so sure her feather was right and that Chip was wrong. Still, he decided not to argue. "The main thing right now is to put some distance between us and the Titans. Let's go!" he yelled.

Poseidon and Artemis jumped to Hera's side at last. Together, they steered up the coast as the Titans' winds rocked the boat like a baby's cradle. Big waves crashed against the sides, spilling onto the deck.

"Athena, Demeter, Hephaestus, Apollo, get into the hold!" Zeus commanded. Those four Olympians had been hanging on to the sides of the deck. He feared they were in danger of falling off. They didn't have as much experience with sea travel as the other six Olympians did.

"Make a chain!" Athena called over the wind, and the four of them held hands as they made their way safely belowdecks.

Zeus gripped one of the masts and stared up at the battle still raging in the sky. As the winds and waves continued, their ship creaked and groaned. The Olympians still on deck struggled to keep from falling over.

"We're going to be broken into toothpicks!" Poseidon wailed over the howling storm.

"You're the ruler of the seas!" Hera called to him. "Can't you do something to calm things down?"

"This isn't the ocean's fault!" Poseidon shot back. "It's those two Titan windbags who are stirring things up!"

Ares gripped his spear. "Why are we running away? We should fight them," he said fiercely. "We can take them! I'll show them what—"

Just then a huge wave smacked into him, knocking him over and soaking him. He spat out the salt water and scowled.

"Hang on!" Zeus cried out, studying the coastline they were fast approaching. Then he looked at Hera. "Where are we supposed to land?"

"I don't know!" she yelled back, peering over the side of the ship. "My feather didn't say—"

Another punishing wave hit the ship. This one picked them up like a huge, watery fist and carried them toward shore at a dangerous speed.

"Steer away!" Zeus yelled. But he was too late. Things started to happen fast. Hera and Poseidon were thrown overboard! Their ship ran aground on the beach. The rest of the Olympians cried out in shock and fear as their ship keeled over to lie on its side in the sand.

"Whoa!" Zeus lost the grip he'd taken on the mast and slid down the deck. When his feet hit the railing, he stopped and swung over the side of the ship to the sand below.

Hera and Poseidon swam up onshore, drenched. Ares, Artemis, Hestia, and Hades scrambled over the rails to drop down beside Zeus. Athena, Demeter, Hephaestus, and Apollo rushed out of the hold to follow them off the ship.

"Is everyone okay?" Zeus asked once they all stood on the beach.

"Oh, great! A shipwreck!" Hephaestus grumped as the others nodded wearily. "This is all we need." Gripping the cane he used to walk, he stumbled across the sand. When he came to a halt by the others, he went uncharacteristically quiet as he took in the smashed ship.

"You were shipwrecked when you were little," Athena remembered gently. "That's how you hurt your leg, right?"

"Oh, this must bring back bad memories for you," Hestia offered kindly.

"It does!" blustered Hephaestus. "And if *I'd* been in charge, we wouldn't have crashed." He sent Zeus a dark glance.

Zeus ignored him. Hephaestus had made it clear plenty of times that he wanted to lead the Olympians. And sometimes Zeus would have loved to pass his leadership responsibilities to someone else. But leading Olympians wasn't a job you chose—it was a job that chose you. And Pythia had said that Zeus had been chosen, whether he liked it or not.

"Well, at least we got away from the Titans," Hera pointed out.

"Are you kidding?" Hades asked. "Have you looked up lately?"

All the Olympians glanced up at the dark sky. Uranus's giant body still stretched from one end of the horizon to the other. Just then a new volley of stars and rocks rained down on them like hail.

"Take cover!" Zeus yelled. He scanned the area as they turned to move inland. Maybe there was a cave somewhere, or at least a rocky overhang.

Quickly, Apollo called them back, pointing out to sea. *"I know you want to escape Titan troubles, but shouldn't we wait for those incoming bubbles?"* he sing-songed.

"Huh?" Zeus spun around to see a huge wave of sparkly bubbles moving in from the sea. It was heading right for them!

CHAPTER FOUR

An Olympian Is Born!

The Olympians stared wide-eyed at the approaching wave of bubbles, which sparkled in glittering shades of gold, pink, and blue. It carried an enormous, perfect shell, as big as a canoe. The bubbles gurgled and bounced around the shell, cushioning it from harm.

"Those bubbles don't look so scary," Demeter remarked.

As the shell got closer, they drew back. "I wonder what's inside the shell, though," said Poseidon.

"Careful! A Creature of Chaos could be hiding in there!" Zeus exclaimed. Who knew if the shell was carrying a friend or foe?

The waves deposited the shell on the shore and then withdrew back into the churning sea. Long seconds passed. The scallop shell sat there on the sand. Eventually, the Olympians took a few cautious steps toward it. It was hinged on one side and looked like a giant clamshell.

Suddenly, the shell popped open. "What's in it?" asked Artemis, who was in the back of the group and couldn't see.

"It's a girl!" said Hephaestus said in surprise.

"Shh! Can't you see she's sleeping?" hissed Ares.

Zeus let out a sigh of relief. The girl in the shell didn't appear troublesome at all. She had

long, blond hair that cascaded around her white dress, and she looked to be their age.

"Her hair is so . . . blond," Ares said, his red eyes wide with wonder.

"So? *My* hair is blond," Hera snapped. "Apollo's is too."

"But hers is shinier and, um, blonder," Ares argued.

Zeus couldn't help rolling his eyes. "Is this really worth an argument?" he asked Hera and Ares. Could Hera be jealous of the shell girl? he wondered. She was grouchy even in the best of times, but her grouchiness grew worse whenever she was feeling jealous.

Before either could reply, Apollo burst into song. *"A blond girl in a shell has come from the sea. Now all must wonder, who exactly is she?"*

Zeus glanced over his shoulder at Poseidon. "Do you know her?"

The ruler of the sea shook his head. "Nope. Never seen her before." There was a goofy lovey-dovey look on his face.

Hephaestus took a step closer to the shell. For the first time since they had boarded the ship, he wasn't scowling. He had the same look on his face as Poseidon did. Come to think of it, Ares and the other guys did too.

"She's . . . *amazing,*" Hephaestus said dreamily. "More amazing than any creature I ever created in Lemnos."

"Well, of course she is. She's probably a mortal, not one of your dumb machines," Hera pointed out.

Yes, definitely jealous, decided Zeus.

"If she's a mortal, she's no ordinary one," said the gray-eyed Athena, walking around the shell to study the girl.

"Maybe she really is a Creature of Chaos!" Hera crowed.

Ares snorted. "No way! Does she look like a monster to you?"

"A monster doesn't always *look* like a monster, you know," Hera insisted. "Haven't you heard that beauty's only skin deep? Monsters can look nice, but act mean."

Just then Demeter gasped and pointed at the girl in the shell. "Look!"

A silence fell as the girl slowly opened her eyes. They were blue, but not just any old blue, Zeus noted. They were the color of tropical ocean waters, with flecks of gold, like sunlight, in them. Then she smiled, showing off perfect bright white teeth that practically blinded the Olympians.

"Hello!" she said cheerfully.

"Hello!" they all greeted her back. Ares's and Hephaestus's voices were loudest.

"We're Olympians. And you are?" Hera asked pointedly.

The girl sat up inside her shell. "My name is . . ." She paused and then giggled, as if trying to remember it. Then she said, "Oh, yeah. Aphrodite. I am the most beautiful girl you have ever seen!"

Hera and the other girls looked at one another and frowned. Talk about vain! But the boys couldn't take their eyes off the new girl—not even Zeus.

Maybe Hera's right after all, Zeus thought. *This girl has to be some kind of magical creature. It is like she's cast a spell on them! Well, on the boys, anyway.*

As Aphrodite stood, Hephaestus and Ares rushed forward to help her step onto the shore. "The sand is so . . . soft!" she said, her voice filled with awe. Then she looked up. "And the sky is so . . . big! It makes me feel tiny!" She giggled again, and Zeus thought her laugh sounded like the sweetest bells he'd ever heard.

Aphrodite began to prance around the beach. "The breeze! It's so cool, it makes me want to dance! Is it always this wonderful?"

"It's plain old Titan-made stormy wind," said Hera flatly. "What's so wonderful about that?"

Aphrodite's eyes sparkled. "It's wonderful because it's new!"

Athena's gray eyes narrowed. "What do you mean 'new'? Have you been trapped in that shell for ten years?"

Aphrodite shook her head. "Of course not, silly!" Then she giggled again and ran up to Athena's aegis, a bright, golden shield that hung around Athena's neck.

Aphrodite peered into the shiny shield as if it were a mirror. "Ooh, I can see myself! I really *am* pretty, aren't I?"

Athena's aegis—along with her Thread of Cleverness—made her pretty good at figuring out mysteries. And Aphrodite was definitely a mystery. Athena quickly realized what was up with the girl. "I think Aphrodite was just born," she announced.

Zeus shook his head. "Huh? That makes no sense. She looks the same age as us!"

Athena glanced over at Aphrodite. The girl had picked up a seashell and was holding it to her ear, listening intently to the sound of the "sea" inside it.

"Aphrodite, today's your first day alive, isn't it?" Athena asked.

Aphrodite pulled the shell away from her ear and nodded. "Yes, my very first day. And it's awesome!" Then she looked up at the sky and pouted. "I don't like the dark sky, though, and the icky sharp things falling from it. When will they stop?"

"This is crazy," Artemis said, shaking her head. "Nobody is already ten years old when they're born!"

"Uh-huh. And nobody lives in the belly of a giant Titan like Cronus for ten years either," Poseidon pointed out. "But some of us Olympians did."

"And she's acting like someone just born," Athena added. "Which means she's like a walking, talking baby, and we need to protect her."

"I'll do it!" said Ares and Hephaestus at the same time. Both boys flexed their muscles, posing in strong, protective stances.

Zeus motioned to Poseidon and Hades, and the three brothers huddled together. "Pythia said we had to find the bubbles, so there must have been a reason," Zeus told them. "That wave of bubbles brought Aphrodite to us. She's our age, and she—"

"She's weird, just like the rest of us," Poseidon interrupted.

"Speak for yourself! Just because I rule the dead and my pet is a dog with three heads, that doesn't make *me* weird," Hades said. Then he thought about it. "Oh wait, maybe it does."

"The point is that our quest is over," said Zeus. "Plus, I think the bubbles led us to a new O—"

Just then Hestia came over and tapped him on the shoulder. "So, we girls think Aphrodite is an Olympian," she announced.

"Yeah! That's what I was just trying to say," said Zeus.

"Wha—?" said Ares and Hephaestus, overhearing. They'd been "protecting" Aphrodite while the others had begun sweeping away any sharp-edged stones or shells they found around her so that she wouldn't accidentally step on them and hurt her feet.

"The girl from the shell is an Olympian as well," sang Apollo.

"But that was too easy!" Poseidon exclaimed. "Usually, we have to fight Creatures of Chaos on a quest."

"And get chased by Cronies," Hades reminded them.

"And if our quest is over, where's Pythia?" asked Ares. The oracle always appeared to them at the end of each quest to congratulate the Olympians for completing it and to tell them about their next quest.

"You mean that lady with the foggy specs?" asked Hephaestus.

Apollo rolled his eyes. "She's an *oracle*. She can see into the future."

"Really? Then why didn't she tell us we were going to get stuck in the middle of a father-and-son Titan fight and get shipwrecked?" Hephaestus asked.

"Can we please focus, people?" Hera asked. "Before something happens to your precious Aphrodite."

Turned out that the bubbly girl had wandered away while the others were talking. Now she was picking bright-red berries from a bush farther down the shore. Zeus rushed over to her.

"Stop!" he said. "Those are poisonous. They'll make you sick."

Ares glared at Hephaestus. "Nice job protecting her."

"Ditto!" Hephaestus shot back.

Aphrodite's beautiful ocean-blue eyes went wide. "But I'm so hungry!"

"Me too." Hera held up her feather and studied it. "There's a village nearby. Let's go see if we can scrounge some food."

"I'll walk by Aphrodite," said Ares quickly.

"No, I will!" said Hephaestus, and the two boys bumped into each other, trying to get to Aphrodite first.

Zeus sighed. Finding another Olympian had been lucky. But he had a feeling that the girl from the bubbles was going to add to their troubles!

CHAPTER FIVE

Still Hungry!

C hip, can you get us to the village?" Zeus asked his amulet.

"Es-yip!" Chip replied, and a black arrow formed on the surface of the smooth stone to point the way.

"Okay, let's get going!" Zeus called out to the others loudly. "Make sure you have everything you need from the ship."

As the Olympians gathered up their packs

and got ready to leave, the sky above them grew brighter. Aphrodite shielded her eyes from the sun. "Ooh, it's turning prettier and prettier!" she cried.

"Looks like Uranus is leaving," remarked Athena.

She was right. A few minutes later, the Titan was completely gone, leaving behind a bright-blue sky with a slowly sinking sun.

"I wonder who won the fight—him or Cronus?" Ares asked.

"Who cares?" Zeus answered. He wouldn't have rooted for either of them to win! But at least while his father and grandfather were fighting, they'd been too busy to bother destroying the Olympians.

"It'll be dark for real soon, though." Hestia held up her magical object, a torch. "I can light this if I need to, but we should get moving."

With Zeus in the lead they began to march inland, following Chip's arrow. Hephaestus and Ares guarded Aphrodite, who danced rather than walked along the path. Tiny, sparkly bubbles bobbed around her with every step. The other Olympians made a game of chasing and popping them. For a while their spirits remained high.

"How far is this village?" Hephaestus complained after a while. The sky had grown darker as they walked, and this time Uranus wasn't the cause. It really was almost night.

"Well?" Zeus asked Chip.

"Hree-tip ours-hip," Chip replied.

"'Three hours'?" Poseidon translated. "It'll be pitch black before then!"

"We'd better find a place to camp," Athena suggested.

Zeus nodded. After another hour of walking

they found a clearing next to a stream. Everyone dug into their packs and pulled out whatever olives, stale bread, and berries they had left.

Poseidon frowned. "All of our bread is soggy. Too bad we didn't get a chance to go fishing."

"It'll have to do for now," said Zeus. "We'll get better food in the village tomorrow."

They all settled in and soon fell asleep after they ate, exhausted. As they slept, shiny bubbles danced around Aphrodite in the moonlight.

In the morning they all drank water from the creek and then eagerly headed for the village. It wasn't long before they saw a dozen huts stretched across low, grassy hills. Each hut had a fenced-in yard with chickens, goats, or large, brown cows. Crops grew in a nearby field, and a stream ran between the field and the huts.

"All right," Zeus said. "Looks like there's plenty of food here. What do we have to trade?"

"Weapons?" Hera suggested.

Ares hugged his pack and glared at Hera. "You're not taking any of mine!"

"Actually, they're mostly *my* weapons, remember? We took them from *my* island on your last quest," Hephaestus said pointedly.

"We won't need many for trade," Athena reassured Ares. "A slingshot or some extra arrows should buy us enough to eat for a few days."

While the others searched their packs for weapons to trade for food, Aphrodite walked to the edge of the village's stream. There, she saw a girl dragging a fishing net through the water.

"What are you doing?" Aphrodite asked her.

The girl seemed surprised by the question, but she couldn't help smiling at Aphrodite. "Fishing," she replied.

"My friend Poseidon likes fish too!" Aphrodite exclaimed. "You should be his girlfriend!"

Poseidon had left his pack on the ground to follow Aphrodite when he saw her leave, so he was right behind her when she said this. He turned bright red. "Girlfriend? But I'm only ten years old!"

Aphrodite giggled. "Just kidding," she teased. Apparently, though she'd only been born yesterday, she was already learning to joke.

Just then a young farmer walked up to them. "Can I help you, travelers?" he asked.

Zeus nodded and held up a handful of arrows. "We'd like to trade weapons for some food."

The farmer raised his eyebrows. "Sure, we've got food, but do you mind if I ask what you kids are doing traveling around with weapons?"

"We're not mortal kids," Hera answered him. "We're Olympians." She gave him a proud smile.

A look of wonder came over the farmer's face.

"Really? You're the kids who are going to take down King Cronus, right? The ones everyone's talking about. In that case, you can have all the food you want. For free!"

As the Olympians let out a cheer, Aphrodite ran over. "What's everyone so happy about?"

"We're getting food!" Hades reported.

A young woman wearing her hair in a long braid came toward them now, and the farmer motioned her over. "Alysa, these kids are the Olympians!" he called out.

The woman smiled. "Really? That's so cool!"

Aphrodite stared first at the farmer and then at the young woman. "Are you his girlfriend?" she asked.

Alysa nodded, blushing. "Yes, Eli and I are to be married next month."

Aphrodite shook her head. "Oh, that's too bad."

Alysa's smile faded. "What do you mean?"

"You're not right for each other," Aphrodite said sweetly. "You should break up before it's too late."

"What? But I love Eli!" Alysa protested.

"And I love you," Eli said to her. But then he looked at Aphrodite. "So . . . you're an Olympian. Does that mean you have some magical way of seeing into our future?"

Alysa frowned at him. "Who cares if she does?"

"Just asking," Eli said lightly. "Maybe she knows something we should be aware of, and . . ."

"Ha!" Alysa spat out. She spun around and glared at Aphrodite. "Why are you trying to cause trouble here?"

Aphrodite looked at her in innocent surprise. "I'm just trying to help. I seem to have a knack for, um, matchmaking."

"Well, I think you stink at matchmaking.

In fact, I don't think you're an Olympian at all," said Alysa. Her eyes narrowed as she scanned the faces of the other Olympians. "I think you're all just a bunch of phonies looking to get free food! Make them leave, Eli!" she ordered.

Eli sighed. "You guys had better go. Sorry I couldn't help."

"Nooo!" wailed Poseidon, rubbing his empty belly.

Zeus pulled him away. "Let's go. We're in enough trouble with the Titans. We don't need to get mortals mad at us too." He'd had a feeling Aphrodite might cause trouble, and now she had.

With Zeus in the lead as usual, the hungry Olympians marched out of the village. Hephaestus hurried to keep pace. As he moved along, the cane slid outward, causing Zeus to fall.

Unharmed, Zeus leaped up. It almost seemed

like the guy had tripped him on purpose. "Can't you control that thing?" Zeus asked him.

"Can't *you* control your followers?" Hephaestus shot back. "Because if you could, we would have gotten some food back there."

Before Zeus could reply, Hera jumped to his defense, surprising him. "Maybe it's your fault we don't have that food, Hephaestus. Maybe if you and Ares had kept Aphrodite *under control*, our stomachs wouldn't still be growling."

"Are we supposed to put a hand over her mouth every time she opens it or something?" Ares grumped.

Hephaestus nodded at Zeus. "Yeah. Don't blame us. You should have smoothed that situation over. A *real* leader would have."

Zeus ignored him and stomped onward along the path.

Seconds later, Hera released her feather to fly

ahead. When it returned she looked into its eye. "There's another village right over the hill," she reported.

The Olympians quickly reached this second village, which looked a lot like the first one. Only this time, someone was standing in their path waiting for them.

It was a young woman with pale, white skin and thick, black hair that fell in long, twisted braids down her back. She wore a long, black dress. And though she smiled at the Olympians, her smile was a crafty one.

"Welcome, travelers. I am Eris!" the woman said. "May I offer you some food?"

CHAPTER SIX

The House of Eris

Yes!" cried Poseidon. In an instant he bounded down the path to meet her. The other Olympians followed—except for Athena and Zeus. The two of them hung back to talk.

"Eris. I know that name from somewhere," Athena said in a low voice. Fixing her eyes on Eris's back as the woman led the others away, Athena nervously twisted her Thread of Cleverness around her finger.

"Hmm. Doesn't ring a bell," said Zeus. "But she seems friendly."

"Maybe too friendly," Athena added.

"Yeah," Zeus whispered. "But our odds are good if she tries anything. Twelve of us against one of her. And I'm hungry!"

Up ahead, Apollo was singing a new song he'd made up as they followed Eris along the path. *"Eris is going to give us some food. This is putting us in a good mood."*

"Fine, we'll eat her food. But let's keep our eyes peeled," Athena said. "I don't know what she's up to, but I don't trust her."

"You and me both," said Zeus before they joined the other Olympians.

Eris led them to a cottage with a high roof. She opened the door. "Come inside. I have prepared you a feast." Behind her house stretched a dark, quiet forest.

Inside, Zeus and Athena exchanged a look of alarm when they saw the dining table set with twelve places. "How did you know we were coming?" Zeus demanded.

But Eris ignored his question, and the other Olympians were so hungry, they didn't feel suspicious. Without hesitation, they'd rushed toward the table filled with food.

"Bread! Cheese! Figs! And are those chicken legs?" Poseidon asked, practically drooling.

"Please have a seat," said Eris, gesturing toward the chairs around the table. There were exactly twelve of them. "Start right in. I know you must be hungry. But if you'll excuse me, I have something I need to see to," she said with another crafty smile. "Be back soon."

Sweeping past Zeus and Athena, she strode

from the room. The other Olympians quickly pulled out the chairs and sat down, but Zeus and Athena were more cautious.

"Stop eating!" Zeus called, racing for the table now that Eris was gone. "That food could be poison for all we know!"

Poseidon had just gulped down a fig whole. "Poison? Now you tell me!"

Zeus looked at Chip. "Is this food safe to eat?" he asked.

"Es-yip," Chip replied. At this, Poseidon heaved a sigh of relief and heaped more food onto his plate. When Athena went to sit at one end of the table, between Hera and Aphrodite, Zeus took the only other open seat at the opposite end of the table. He still didn't trust Eris, but it would probably be easier to outwit her on a full stomach. He put some chicken, figs, and cheese on his plate and began to eat.

Glancing down the table he saw that Poseidon had now piled his plate higher than the top of his head!

"You might have saved some for the rest of us!" Hera scolded him, though her plate looked plenty full to Zeus.

"Stop worrying" came Poseidon's voice from beyond the mound. "There's plenty for every-body."

"It's so nice to eat warm, soft bread instead of the stale kind," remarked Demeter, who was across the table from Poseidon.

Athena picked up one her olives and popped it in her mouth. "Mmm."

"It's all awesome!" agreed Hephaestus. He took a huge bite out of a chicken drumstick. With his mouth full, he added, "Thish ish uh feesh fish fuhr uh Olympuh kink!"

Zeus wasn't sure, but he thought Hephaestus

had said, "This is a feast fit for an Olympic king." Was that how Hephaestus saw himself, as king of the Olympians? As Zeus's replacement? Bubbles were still floating around Aphrodite at the far end of the table. Hera kept waving them away as they floated over her plate. "You're getting bubbles on my food!' she complained.

Aphrodite giggled. "I can't help it. They do as they please."

"*I'll* follow you wherever you go," Ares blurted out, and then he blushed. "Did I just say that out loud?"

"You sure did, Bro," Poseidon said, shaking his head as if embarrassed for Ares.

They'd just about finished eating when Eris returned at last. "I have something to show you," she announced. There was a pause as their gazes swung her way. Her eyes shone (*mischievously*, Zeus thought) as she strode toward them.

"And now for the best part of the meal," she said. With dramatic flair she extended her right hand toward the table. "Ta-da!" she exclaimed. A bright, golden apple glittered in her palm.

"It's a gift for the fairest among you," she explained. Then she set the apple onto the table and gave it a little push. "Here you go."

The apple slowly rolled down the table, past the plates of food, and came to a stop right between Athena, Aphrodite, and Hera!

CHAPTER SEVEN

Who's the Fairest?

Apollo, who was sitting by Hera, reached for the golden apple. "I think it's plain to see, that the fairest of us is me," rhymed the blond-haired, blue-eyed boy.

Hera slapped Apollo's hand away. "No way! Eris was talking about one of us girls."

"Yes," Aphrodite agreed. "Girls are *fair*. Boys are *handsome*."

"But which girl?" Poseidon asked, and his question hung in the air.

"Who did you mean the apple for, Eris?" Zeus asked, sensing that trouble was brewing. But he turned just in time to see their strange host disappear. As she glided from the room, he noticed feathers poking out of the back of her sleeveless dress.

"Feathers!" he hissed to Athena as the other Olympians continued arguing around them. "I think Eris has wings!"

Athena's eyes narrowed. "That's it!" she exclaimed. "I just remembered why her name is familiar. Eris is the winged goddess of discord!"

"Discord?" Zeus asked. "As in disagreement and conflict? And in making Olympians argue?"

Athena nodded worriedly. "She's a Creature of Chaos. She can even cause wars!"

"That apple is obviously meant for Aphrodite,"

Hephaestus was saying now. "She's clearly the prettiest one here—prettiest in the whole world, even."

"Yeah. Like he said!" Ares echoed.

Aphrodite started to reach for the apple but drew her hand back when Hera snapped at her. "Leave it!" Hera glared at Aphrodite's two supporters. "What do you two know, anyway?

"Yeah, Hephaestus. You lived on an island full of hairy guys most of your life," said the normally good-tempered Athena. "And, Ares, your best friends were a flock of metal birds."

"Well, since Eris isn't here to ask who the apple is meant for, I suppose we should just leave it on the table and be on our way," Zeus said. Eris was obviously trying to start trouble among them with this apple. If he didn't stop it, who knew what could happen?

However, before anyone could second his

suggestion, Aphrodite grabbed the apple. "Since I am very pretty, I should be the one to take it." She batted her long eyelashes at the group.

Hera looked at her sisters, Hestia and Demeter. "Can you believe she just said that? I mean, I'm pretty too, but I don't go around saying it."

"But you just did say it!" argued Hades.

Zeus jumped up. "We should just leave the apple and go," he commanded. "I couldn't eat another bite!"

"I could," Poseidon said. His plate was empty. It was so clean, he must have licked it. Now he began heaping more food on it.

Gesturing a hand at Zeus, Hephaestus snorted and spoke to the others. "There's your leader, running away again! I'll show you what a leader really should do. Make decisions. And *I* have decided that Aphrodite should get the apple!"

"You're *not* our leader," Hera snapped. "And

the apple landed closest to me, Aphrodite, and Athena, so it could belong to any one of us."

"I bet it's for you, Hera," said Hestia.

"Yes, I vote for Hera to get the apple," agreed Demeter.

"'Fair' does not have to mean a pretty face. It could also mean someone who is just and has grace," rhymed Apollo. "I think Athena should get the apple."

Athena beamed. "Thank you," she said, but then she frowned. "Wait, are you saying I'm not pretty?"

Apollo began to sing. *"You are as pretty as can be, but perhaps not as pretty as Aphro—"*

"Wait! Don't finish that, dude!" Zeus blurted out.

"Well, I think Athena has nice eyes," Hades offered. "Gray is one of my favorite colors. It reminds me of the fog in the Underworld."

Athena folded her arms across her chest.

"Huh? That does not sound like a compliment!"

Hephaestus shook his cane to get the Olympians' attention and accidentally knocked over a bowl of gravy in the process. "Quiet, everyone!" he shouted. "I'm sure we can work this out. Let me think."

Zeus grinned and folded his arms. Ha! Let Hephaestus see how easy it was to be the leader of the Olympians. *Not!*

"Well, if we're judging the fairest by eye color," Poseidon said heatedly to Hades, "then Aphrodite would win hands down. Because her eyes are the color of the sea!"

Zeus glanced around the table. By now, *everyone* was arguing! He thought quickly. What would Eris's object be in making the Olympians argue?

To weaken us, of course, he realized. With the hope that they'd split apart. Then they'd be less of a threat to the Titans, who must have sent this goddess of discord to intercept them. He had to put a stop to this! If only he could get the others to listen. To follow him. Suddenly, he figured out a way. He grabbed the golden apple from the table and ran outside.

Sure enough, the other eleven Olympians followed him. Luckily, there was no sign of Eris. So he just kept running. He didn't stop till he had reached the edge of a village. When he spotted a handsome and finely dressed teenage boy riding toward him on his horse, Zeus stopped and waited for everyone to catch up. Once they did, they began arguing again.

"Listen! I have an idea!" he called over the loud voices. "Let's ask somebody who's not an Olympian to decide who gets the apple. Someone like this guy." He pointed at the teenage boy.

"That sounds fair," said Poseidon. The others

murmured their agreement as well.

"Good. That's settled, then," said Zeus.

"Excuse me!" he said, running up to the boy on the horse. "We're Olympians. Do you think you could help us?"

The boy smiled a dazzling smile—almost as dazzling as Aphrodite's. He had wavy brown hair and green eyes, and his white tunic and trousers were embroidered with gold stitching.

"Sure," he said, dismounting from his horse. "I am Prince Paris of Troy. How can I help?"

Hera took a step forward and smiled big at him. "We want you to decide which one of us is the fairest," she said, pointing first at herself and then, in turn, at Athena and Aphrodite.

"The one you choose wins this golden apple," Zeus said, handing it to Paris.

Paris looked at the apple and then at the three girls. "Well, that's a tough decision. I don't really know you girls, but I'm sure each of you is fair in your own way."

Zeus started to get worried. He had hoped Paris would just quickly pick one. Then this foolishness would end and they could all head peacefully off.

"Maybe I can make your choice easier," Hera said. Her smile widened, and she held up her feather. "My feather is magic. I can look into its eye and tell you your future."

"Hey, that's a bribe!" Athena complained.

"I don't remember any rule against bribes," Hera pointed out.

Athena glared at her. "Well, if bribes are okay, then I have something even better for you, Paris." She turned to the prince and held up her Thread of Cleverness. "How would you like a piece of this? It'll make you as wise as an owl."

Paris looked thoughtful. "Those are both

very good offers," he said slowly.

Zeus frowned. It really wasn't like Athena to act this way. Especially when she knew that Eris had been trying to stir up trouble. And since when was Hera a cheater? Since they'd met the goddess of discord, that's when!

Before Zeus could come up with a way to fix things, they heard barking.

Arf! Arf! A furry brown puppy came running down the path, chasing a butterfly and happily yapping away.

Paris gazed at it with adoring eyes. "How about if I just give the golden apple to that puppy?" he asked with a huge grin. "She's the cutest thing I've ever seen!"

Aphrodite scooped up the puppy as she tried to run by her. She cuddled the little dog in her arms. She gave Aphrodite sloppy puppy kisses all over her face.

"She's yours if you want her," Aphrodite said with a giggle. Then, with a smile as crafty as Eris's, she added, "All you have to do is give me the apple!"

CHAPTER EIGHT

Bolt, Where Are You?

t's yours!" Paris cried happily. Aphrodite gave him the puppy and plucked the golden apple from his hand. The little brown dog rained kisses all over her new owner.

Paris turned to Zeus. "Thanks! This was fun." Cradling the puppy under one arm, he rode off.

Once the prince was gone, Zeus glanced around at Athena, Hera, and Aphrodite. "Bribery? Really? The world expects better of Olympians."

While Athena and Hera had the decency to look a little ashamed of their actions, Aphrodite seemed clueless. She was playing with the apple now, giggling as she tossed it up in the air and then caught it. Zeus was beginning to wonder if she was as bubbleheaded as the bubbles that constantly floated around her.

Hephaestus waved his cane. "Who cares? Aphrodite has the apple, just like I said she should."

With a stormy look on her face, Hestia stomped over to him. The fire in the torch she carried flamed high. *Uh-oh*, thought Zeus. It seemed angry, just like her.

"Let's get this straight," the normally calm and easygoing Hestia said to Hephaestus. "You are *not* the boss of us! And I *still* say that Hera should get the apple."

Whoa, thought Zeus. He'd hoped Paris's

decision would put this whole contest thing behind them now that Aphrodite had the apple. Even if she hadn't won it fair and square.

"But Hera's the one who started the bribing in the first place," Hephaestus pointed out.

"Just let Aphrodite keep it!" Ares chimed in. "She really is the fairest, anyway."

"You boys stay out of it!" Demeter complained.

Artemis shook her head. "Choosing who's the prettiest is dumb, anyway. We should have an archery contest to win the apple."

Hera spun around. "Why, so you can win?"

"Why not a math contest, instead," Athena suggested. "Or a history contest." Which of course were contests a brainy girl like her could easily win.

Apollo strummed his lyre. *We'll never decide if we yell and shout. Perhaps instead we all should fight it out.*

"Good plan!" Ares cheered.

Hephaestus shook his head. "Are you sure you guys are really Olympians? Because you're acting like a bunch of babies."

Finally, Zeus had had enough. "Just stop arguing, everybody!" he yelled. "At this rate we really will be fighting one another soon, and it won't be pretty." But nobody paid any attention to him. They went right on arguing.

A thunderstorm will cool everyone down, he decided. He reached to pull Bolt out from his belt. But Bolt wasn't there!

Zeus groaned as he remembered tossing his thunderbolt up into the sky at Cronus and Uranus. How could he not have noticed that Bolt had never come back to him! "Bolt, return!" he called out now. But his magical object did not return.

"Chip, help me find Bolt!" Zeus cried frantically. Normally, if he called Bolt's name, Bolt was back in a flash. Something must be wrong.

A green arrow appeared on Chip's surface, and Zeus raced off in the direction it was pointing—right into the forest. Behind him, the other Olympians were still feuding. None of them even noticed him go.

He ran and ran as he called for Bolt. Finally, deep inside the forest now, he stopped, his heart pounding. He couldn't keep running after Bolt forever. The Olympians needed him. But *he* needed Bolt! How could he go on without his magical object?

"What now, Chip?" he asked. Before the stone could answer, Zeus heard a loud rustling in the trees. Something was coming toward him—and from the way everything around him was shaking, it was something very, very big.

Zeus froze as Cronus came into view. Leaves stuck out of his Titan father's bushy beard, and his eyes were on fire with anger.

Run! screamed a voice inside Zeus. Without Bolt, he had no chance of defending himself.

But before he could move, Cronus calmed and held up a huge hand. "Stop! I am not here to harm you," his dad said, peering down, down, down at Zeus.

"Oh, really?" Zeus replied, looking up, up, up. "Why should I believe you?"

"Just listen to my offer!" Cronus demanded. "Uranus wants me to destroy you, but that's not what I want. Not anymore, anyway. Of all my children, only you have the strength to rule. With me." Cronus got down on one giant knee. "Those other Olympians are squabbling ninnies. They'd argue over something as silly as a . . . a piece of fruit!"

Fruit! As in a golden apple. His suspicions about Cronus sending Eris to make trouble among them had just been confirmed.

"Why not leave your puny brothers and sisters behind and join me, Zeus."

"Don't you mean 'Barf Boy'?" Zeus shot back.

Cronus chuckled. "'Barf Boy' is just an affectionate nickname . . . Son."

Zeus cocked his head at Cronus. "Really? 'Cause it has never felt very 'affectionate' to me."

"Never mind that now," Cronus said. "Listen up, Zeus. Those other Olympians can do nothing for you. I've seen them arguing with you. They don't appreciate your leadership."

Cronus did have a point. But this evil Titan had asked Zeus to join him before, and Zeus had stayed loyal to the Olympians. So why was Cronus asking him again?

He's growing afraid of us, Zeus realized. *He thinks this is the only way he can keep us from eventually defeating him. In that case, maybe I should play along. . . .*

"I will consider your offer," Zeus said carefully. "But only if you let me speak with my mother first!"

Though Cronus was keeping Rhea captive, she had crept away whenever she could to help the Olympians. Zeus had spoken with her under cover of darkness, but he had never seen her face.

Cronus stroked his beard, thinking over Zeus's request. "Wait here," he said finally.

He stomped off and soon disappeared into the trees. Zeus waited anxiously for several minutes. Finally, he heard rustling again, and softer footsteps than Cronus's.

A beautiful Titan emerged from the trees and walked toward him. Her thick, brown hair was coiled on top of her head, and was topped with a silver crown. She wasn't as tall as Cronus or as mean-looking, either. Her brown eyes were large and kind, and she looked plump and soft and . . . *nice*. Rhea.

"Zeus," she said, and her eyes filled with happy tears. "Cronus has granted us a few moments alone."

Zeus ran to her and wrapped his arms around her legs. She smelled like a combination of roses and freshly baked bread. "Mom," he said, choking back tears.

Rhea kneeled so she was eye to eye with him. "You have grown into such a fine boy, Zeus. Brave and strong and wise."

"Cronus keeps asking me to join him," he told her. "And if I did, I could be with you all the time."

Rhea smiled gently. "We will be together one day, Son. But it cannot be now. You must return to the Olympians. They need you."

"Huh? They never even listen to me anymore!"

Zeus complained. "They're always fighting. And when I do help them, they never appreciate it."

"Being a leader is a thankless job," Rhea said, surprising him.

"You got that right," he muttered. His mom totally understood him!

"But you are more important to them than they yet realize, and you must stick with them. You must lead the Olympians whether it seems they want you to or not."

Zeus nodded slowly. He felt in his heart that his mother was right.

"Come with us," he urged. "We can escape before Cronus—"

Stomp! Stomp!

Zeus fought back tears again as Cronus returned to the clearing. Rhea smiled sadly and stroked his hair. "We will meet again," she promised softly, and then she rose to her feet.

Reluctantly, Zeus stepped back from her.

"Well? Did you convince our boy to join me?" Cronus asked Rhea.

Rhea faked a disappointed sigh and shook her head. "I tried," she fibbed.

"Never!" Zeus yelled up at Cronus. "Not in a Crony-zillion years would I ever do that! You can bug off, you big-bellied bully!" With a grin, he added, "Oh, and I meant that nickname 'affectionately,' *Dad*."

Heart pounding, he tore off as fast as his feet could take him. Cronus pounded behind him. He would surely try to crush Zeus if he caught up!

Zeus was small and quicker, though. He jumped over roots and boulders as he headed for his friends. And then he stopped in his tracks. Because there, stuck in a rock, was a shining, thunderbolt-shaped dagger. Bolt!

Of course! Bolt was unable to pull himself

out of stone on his own. Zeus ran to the rock. With an easy tug, he pulled his thunderbolt out. He was the only one alive who could do that. It was how he'd gotten Bolt in the first place, in the Temple at Delphi.

"Bolt, large!" he yelled. Instantly, the dagger grew as tall as Zeus. Now his thunderbolt sizzled with energy in his hand. It made him feel good—strong and powerful.

Zeus grabbed Chip. "Which way back to the Olympians?" he asked, and the green arrow appeared once more. But instead of following Chip's directions, Zeus went down a different path. After a few paces, he stopped and swung his thunderbolt first at one tree and then another, and yet another farther on. The trees crashed to the forest floor. He hoped this might trick Cronus into thinking he'd gone in this direction.

Finally, he headed off in the true direction

Chip had indicated, toward the Olympians. As he jogged along, Zeus zigzagged among the trees until he broke out of the forest.

He slowed down when he saw a young boy nailing a scroll to a tree. Curious, Zeus stopped. The boy's hazel eyes looked sad as they watched Zeus silently read the scroll.

LOST. One furry brown puppy. The most beautiful puppy in the world. Please return to Menelaus.

Zeus turned to the boy. "Your puppy. Was she brown?"

The boy nodded eagerly. "Have you seen her?"

"Maybe," Zeus said. "My friends found a brown puppy in the village." He couldn't bring himself to tell Menelaus that if it *was* the same puppy, Prince Paris had her now.

"Come with me," he told the boy. "I'll take you to talk to my friends."

"Oh, thank you!" Menelaus said happily. "I got my puppy for my birthday. Her name is Helen, and she's my best friend in the whole world."

Zeus hoped they could find the prince. If Menelaus took the puppy back, maybe Paris would finally decide which Olympian was the fairest and all the fighting among them would stop.

As it turned out they were in luck. When they reached the arguing Olympians, they also found Paris. He hadn't gone far. Having tied his horse to a nearby tree, he was sitting on a rock beside the Olympians, listening to them squabble while happily holding the squirming puppy on his lap.

"Helen!" Menelaus cried. He ran toward the puppy with open arms.

Paris hugged the puppy tight to his chest and eyed Menelaus suspiciously. "Who's Helen?" he asked.

"My puppy," Menelaus explained. "She got lost. Thanks for taking care of her for me." He held out his arms expectantly.

But Paris did not loosen his grip. "Aphrodite found her and gave her to me," he said firmly. "So she's my puppy now. See how much she likes me?"

"No fair!" Menelaus exclaimed. "You can't have her! Helen's mine. She's the winner of the grand-prize trophy for the most beautiful puppy in all of Greece!"

"Sorry, but I'm taking her back to Troy with me," Paris shot back.

Menelaus balled his hands into fists. "You'll give her to me, or I'll make you!" he threatened.

Great, thought Zeus. *Just great.* By bringing Menelaus back with him, he'd made things worse instead of better!

As their exchange grew more heated, the

Olympians stopped arguing with one another and turned to watch Paris and Menelaus. Aphrodite must have heard Paris telling Menelaus that she'd given him the puppy. She ran up to the two boys now, amid a flurry of sparkly bubbles.

"Oh no, this is all my fault!" she said. "I'm sorry, Paris. Since the puppy was running loose, I thought she didn't belong to anyone. Guess I made a mistake. You *have* to give her back to this boy."

"No way!" Paris cried. "I am the Prince of Troy! And Trojans don't do give-backs."

"You're Prince Puppy Stealer, that's who you are!" cried Menelaus.

"And you're lying so hard that your fancy pants are on fire!" Paris yelled.

Startled by the yelling, the puppy squirmed and wiggled her way out of Paris's arms. Then she scampered down the path away from the village.

"Helen!" cried Menelaus and Paris at the same time, and they both chased after her.

CHAPTER NINE

Stuck on Aphrodite

P eople of Greece, help me!" Menelaus called out to the villagers he passed. "The Prince of Troy is trying to steal my puppy!"

Instantly coming to the aid of one of their own, the villagers swarmed onto the path and joined in the chase.

"Come on!" Zeus shouted to the other Olympians. "We started this, so we'd better fix it." This time everyone listened to him, and the Olympians sped after the puppy and the two boys, too.

When they caught up to Paris, he was clutching Helen in his arms and heading toward the sandy coastline. Zeus could see a small sailing ship anchored near the shore that was flying a Trojan flag. It must be waiting to take Paris back to Troy! Paris reached the boat and jumped in.

Menelaus wasn't far behind him. "Don't you dare take Helen!" he yelled.

"Row!" Paris commanded the sailors aboard. They swiftly pushed off from shore.

Menelaus splashed into the water, shaking and sputtering as he realized Paris had gotten away. And taken Helen with him! "I will get you, Paris of Troy!" he yelled. "I will not rest until I get my puppy back!"

Then he spun around. "You!" he snarled,

pointing at Zeus and the Olympians, who were now standing on the sand behind him. "I can't believe you gave *my* puppy away. And to an outsider—a Trojan!"

"It was a mistake," Aphrodite reminded him. "We didn't know she was your puppy."

"Traitors!" Menelaus spat out.

A cry went up among the villagers. "Crush the enemies of Greece!" someone shouted.

"What? We're not enemies of Greece," Zeus protested. "We're trying to *save* Greece!"

But the angry crowd didn't listen. With a mighty roar they rushed toward the Olympians. Zeus turned and shouted an order that he had given to his friends many times before: *"Run!"*

The Olympians dashed up the coastline away from the village. One of the advantages of being ten years old was that they were almost always faster than the grown-ups chasing after them.

Once they had a big lead, Zeus checked Chip. "Any hiding places around here?" he asked the magical stone.

Chip's arrow pointed to a hilly area nearby, and Zeus led the others there. By the time they reached the hills, however, the angry mob had run out of steam and turned back toward their village.

The Olympians stopped, panting. Poseidon flopped onto the grass. "Squishy squids! I hate these high-speed chases!" he complained.

Hades rubbed his belly. "I shouldn't have eaten so much cheese," he groaned. "My stomach aches."

Zeus sighed. "That was a close call."

"None of this would have happened if you hadn't brought Menelaus to us," Hera said with a frown.

Duh. Tell me something I don't know, Zeus

thought. But he wisely held his tongue.

"Where did you disappear to, anyway?" Ares asked.

Zeus hesitated. Should he tell everyone? But somehow he knew he had to. If the Olympians were going to work together, they couldn't have secrets.

"I went to find Bolt," Zeus began. "And Cronus found me. He asked me to leave you guys and rule with him."

Poseidon jumped up. "Bro! I hope you said no."

"Of course I said no," Zeus said, feeling a little bit insulted. Sure, he'd been tempted a teeny-tiny bit, but he would never betray the Olympians. Never!

"But I thought he wanted to destroy you," said Hades. "All of us."

"Maybe Cronus thought that without Zeus, we'd fall apart," guessed Hera.

"Well, we probably would," Hestia said matter-of-factly.

Zeus smiled at her, glad for her support. Then, speaking to everyone, he said, "Cronus sent Eris and her golden apple to destroy us from within by making us fight. He knows that if he separates us, he can defeat us."

Athena nodded. "Makes sense. And it almost worked. For a while there, I was supermad at each and every one of you."

"Then we all agree: The only way we can defeat Cronus and the Titans is if we work together," Zeus said. "And to do that you all need to trust me. Because *I'm* your leader."

He looked squarely at Hephaestus when he said that last part.

The boy shrugged. "You can have the job," he said. "Leading this bunch is like herding wildcats."

"So no more arguments about the apple?" Zeus asked them all.

Nobody objected, but Hera and Athena both glared at Aphrodite, who had been playing with the apple again. She tucked it away and tapped Zeus on the shoulder.

"May I speak with you, please?" she asked.

Zeus nodded, and they stepped aside.

"I really want to be friends with the other girls," Aphrodite said. "But I don't think they like me."

"Here's a suggestion," Zeus said after considering the problem. "Why don't you share the apple with them?"

Aphrodite flashed him her dazzling smile. "What a good idea!"

She approached Hera and Athena. "This should belong to all three of us," she said, holding out the apple. "We can take turns, each owning it for a day. Hera, do you want to go first?"

"Sure," Hera said with a big grin. But when she tried to take the apple from Aphrodite's hand, it wouldn't budge!

Hera's eyes narrowed. "Is this some kind of joke? Because it isn't funny."

"It's not, I swear!" Aphrodite protested. She tossed the apple into her other hand. "See? It's not stuck."

"Let me try," offered Athena. But when she tried to take the apple from Aphrodite, she couldn't do it either. Once again it stuck to Aphrodite's palm.

Hera shook her head. "Maybe *you* were just born yesterday, but *we* weren't. You can't trick us."

"I don't think she's tricking us," Athena said. She tapped her chin, deep in thought. After a moment she said, "I wonder if that apple could be connected to her, and only her, somehow."

Hearing her words, it hit Zeus. "Aphrodite, that golden apple is your magical object!"

As the others murmured things like, "Well, of course!" and "We should have realized it earlier!" and "That explains a lot!"

Aphrodite looked down at the apple in wonder. "It's magical? What can it do?"

"It's up to you to figure that out," Zeus told her.

"Hmm," Aphrodite said, tossing the apple from hand to hand. "It *is* beautiful. But it feels . . . powerful, too. And for some reason I keep wanting to roll it. Like this." She ran a few steps and then stopped, rolling the apple across the ground like a bowling ball.

"Hey, watch it!" Poseidon cried as the apple knocked him off his feet. His arms flailing, he fell backward into Zeus, who fell against Hades, knocking him down too. The boys landed on the grass in a tangled heap.

Hera grinned at Aphrodite. "I think that from now on you and I are going to get along just fine!" Hera said to her. The two of them giggled.

CHAPTER TEN

A War Begins

The twelve Olympians marched away, with nowhere to go and nowhere to stay," sang Apollo as the Olympians hiked up a hill a few hours later.

"That's not very cheerful," Artemis complained. "Couldn't you sing about how we're on an adventure or something?"

"But Pythia hasn't given us our mission. So we might as well stop and all go fishin'," Apollo sang back.

"You don't even like fishing!" his sister reminded him.

Apollo shrugged. "Sometimes you have to go with what rhymes."

"He's got a point, Bolt Breath," Hera said to Zeus. "Shouldn't we stop and wait for Pythia instead of wandering aimlessly?"

"Once word gets out that we were in that village, Cronies will come swarming after us," Zeus replied. "And anyway, I don't think it matters where we are. When Pythia is ready to speak to us, she'll pop up like she always does."

They had reached the top of the hill. Down below they could see a small fleet of Greek warships leaving the coast.

"Uh-oh," said Zeus. "It looks like those Greek ships are heading for Troy."

Ares looked longingly at the ships. "A Trojan war. Cool!"

"Not cool," Hestia scolded him. "People get hurt in wars."

Aphrodite looked sad. "Do you suppose the Greeks and Trojans are going to war because of—"

"No, Aphrodite, they are going to war over a guppy!" a new, disembodied voice said.

"Who said that?" said Aphrodite, looking around. "How do you know my name, whoever you are?"

"Me. And I know many things." A strange mist appeared, and the Olympians could see a figure inside it—a woman with long, dark hair and glasses. It was Pythia, the Oracle from the Temple at Delphi.

"Hi, Pythia!" greeted Zeus. "We were hoping you'd appear. Oh, and I think you meant 'war over a puppy,' not 'a guppy.'"

"Of course," said Pythia. "I knew that. My spectacles just got a little foggy, that's all."

"So, maybe you know this already, but this

war that's starting is sort of our fault," Zeus said. "Cronus sent Eris, the goddess of discord—"

"Yes, I know," Pythia interrupted him. "But there's nothing to be done about that for now. And it's important that you begin your next quest. You must render the cherry cakes harmless!"

"Yum! Finally, a quest for snacks!" Poseidon cheered, raising his trident high.

"Oh, sorry about that. I meant cherry snakes," Pythia corrected.

Zeus turned pale. *Ye gods!* He was terrified of all kinds of snakes, no matter what flavor they were—cherry, lemon, fig. . . .

"But is there really nothing we can do to stop the fight over Helen the puppy?" he asked. "Couldn't we go after the Greeks and try to reason with them somehow? Maybe we could keep the war from happening."

Pythia squinted through her spectacles and

then shook her head. "Sadly, war is what is meant to be between Greece and Troy. In time, you will find yourselves embroiled in that fight," she said. "But for now you must find those cherry snakes. Er." She took off her spectacles, polished their lenses, and perched them back on her nose. "Oh, I see. *Berry* snakes. That's what I meant." Pythia frowned. "Oops! Not berry snakes . . . Hairy snakes! Yes, that's it! Hairy snakes!"

"Eew!" squealed Hestia. "This quest is sounding worse and worse."

"Yeah," said Apollo as Pythia vanished without another word.

"Wait!" Zeus called after her. "Are we supposed to find another Olympian this time too?"

"I hope not!" Demeter put in. "Olympian number thirteen? That could be unlucky!"

But Pythia didn't answer them either way.

"I still don't understand why you all listen to

that weird oracle," Hephaestus said. "I mean, snakes aren't hairy. Everyone knows that."

"Maybe these are wearing wigs?" said Hades, making Aphrodite giggle.

"I wonder if they'll have brown hair like me?" Athena asked with a chuckle.

"No matter! I'll give them a haircut with my spear!" cried Ares.

Soon everyone was laughing.

Zeus smiled and looked up at the clear, blue sky. Despite the coming war, things didn't seem too bad right at this moment. On this quest he had gotten to hug his mom. The Olympians' bellies were full. There were no Cronies in sight. And everyone was in high spirits.

But he knew the calm wouldn't last long. Somewhere, maybe even over the next hill, hairy snakes—or even *scarier* creatures—would be waiting for them!